Logging Truck

Dump Truck

Drop-sided Truck

The author wishes to thank
Foden, Kenworth, Volvo, Mercedes-Benz,
Peterbilt, Lansing Linde, and SMC Euroclamp
for their help and cooperation.

First U.S. edition 1992
First published in Great Britain in 1992 by Walker Books Ltd., London.
ISBN 1-56402-073-8
Library of Congress Catalog Card Number 91-58718
Library of Congress Cataloging-in-Publication information is available.

10 9 8 7 6 5 4 3 2 1

The pictures for this book were done with
black ink and colored markers.

Printed in Hong Kong

Candlewick Press
2067 Massachusetts Avenue
Cambridge, Massachusetts 02140

Bernie DRIVES A TRUCK

by Derek Radford

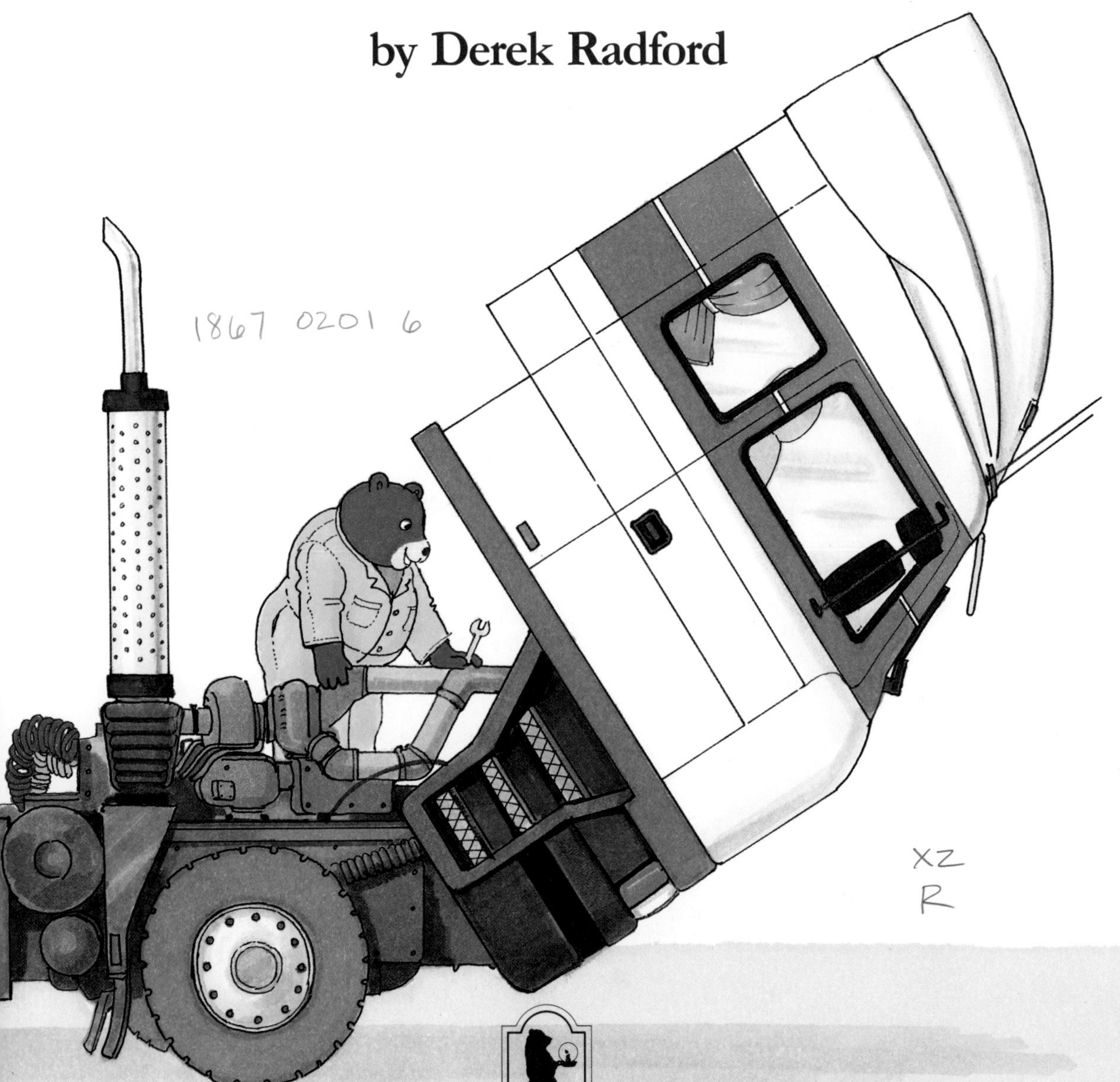

CANDLEWICK PRESS
CAMBRIDGE, MASSACHUSETTS

The alarm rings. Time for Bernie to get up.

The family has breakfast together.

Then Bernie makes lunch to take to work.
The children get ready for school.

“Bye! See you later.”

Bernie checks in at the trucking office to get his job for the day. It's a delivery of soft drinks to the docks.

One driver helps
another check that
his lights are working.

This is Bernie's truck.

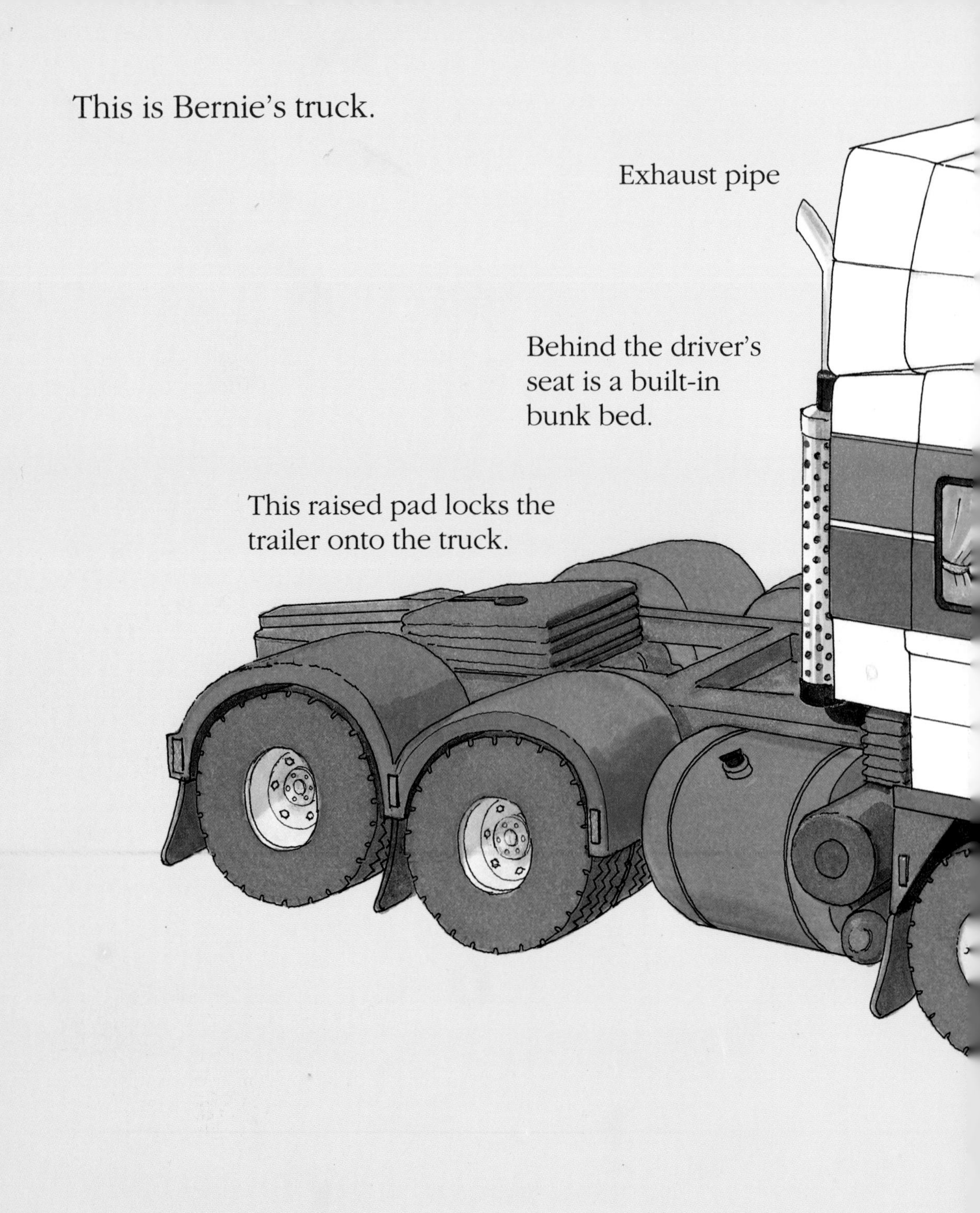

Wing mirrors are heated so they won't fog over.

The windshield has three wipers.

All windows are double-glazed to keep out the cold.

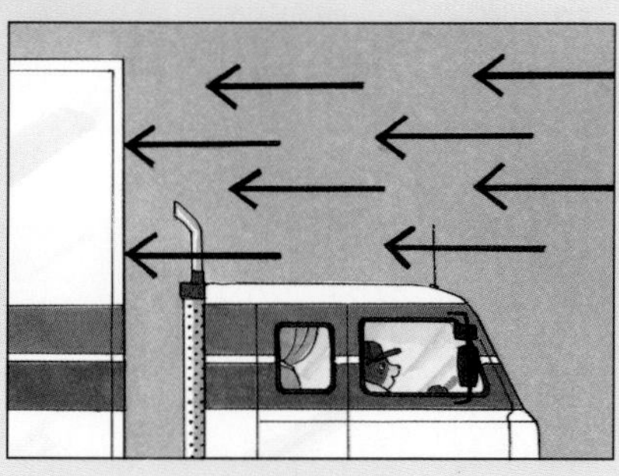

Strong winds pressing against the truck will slow it down.

The air deflector keeps the wind from slowing down the truck too much.

Before he leaves, Bernie checks that all ten tires on his truck have the right amount of air.

Then he fills up with diesel. The fuel tank holds 105 gallons, enough for driving 620 miles.

A mechanic checks the engine, which is underneath the driver's seat.

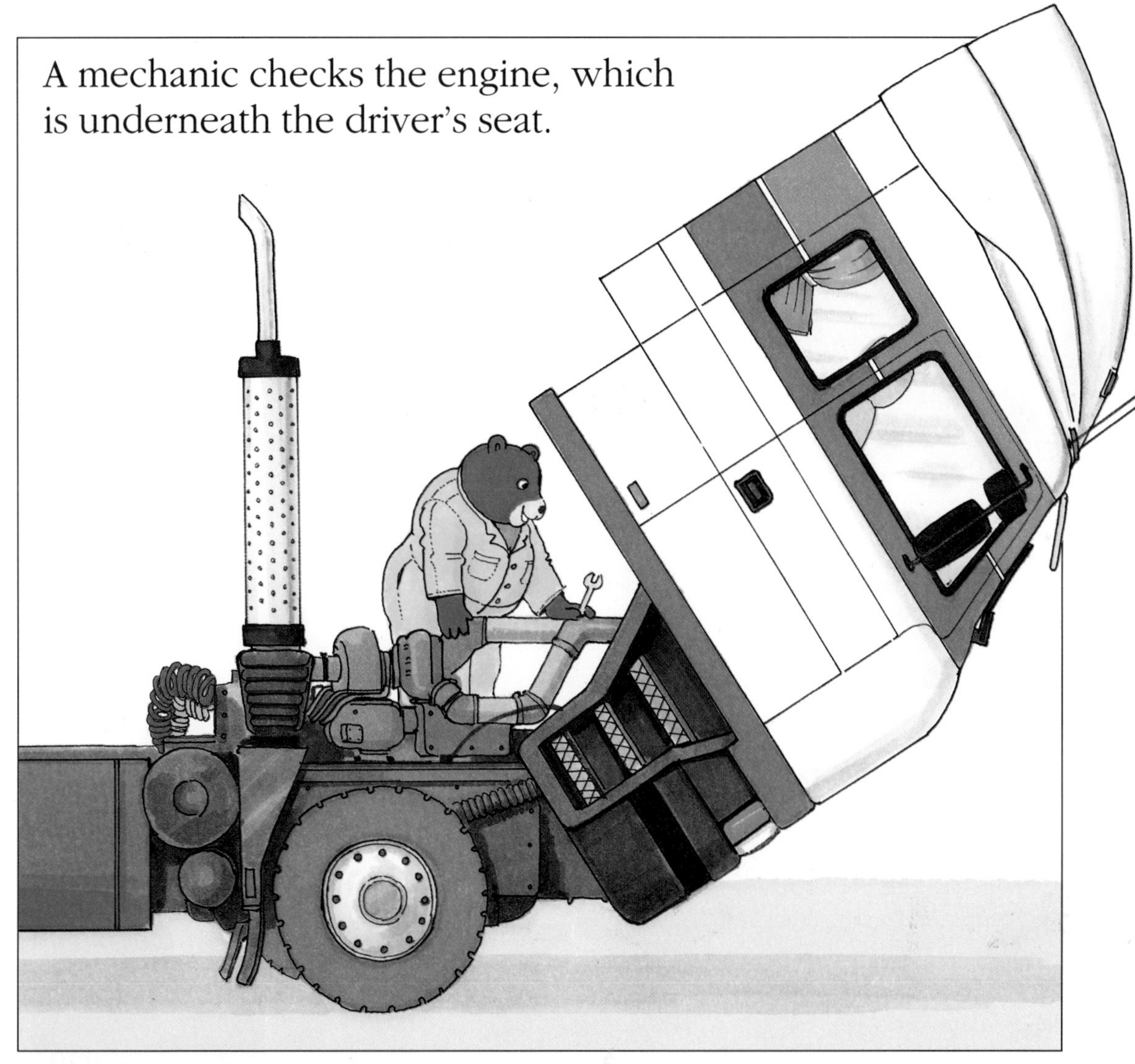

Some of the mechanic's tools:

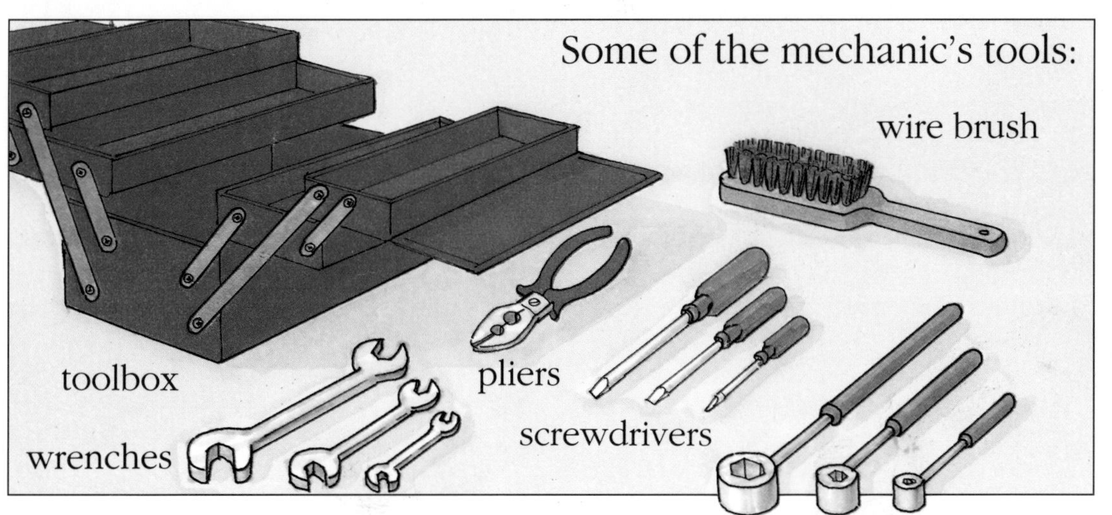

At the soft drink plant, they load up the trailer that Bernie will drive. The cases of soft drinks are very heavy, so they are lifted by a fork lift.

Bernie checks the delivery note to make sure the load isn't too heavy for the truck and trailer.

Everything is ready. The trailer's legs are raised so that Bernie can back his truck under it.

Z 2664

No two delivery trips are the same. This time, after twenty minutes on the road, it starts to rain. Bernie slows down a little. It's dangerous to go too fast on wet roads.

Z 2664

From his seat above the cars, Bernie can see the road ahead clearly. Part of the road is being repaved.

Safe drivers like Bernie always check their wing mirrors and signal before changing lanes.

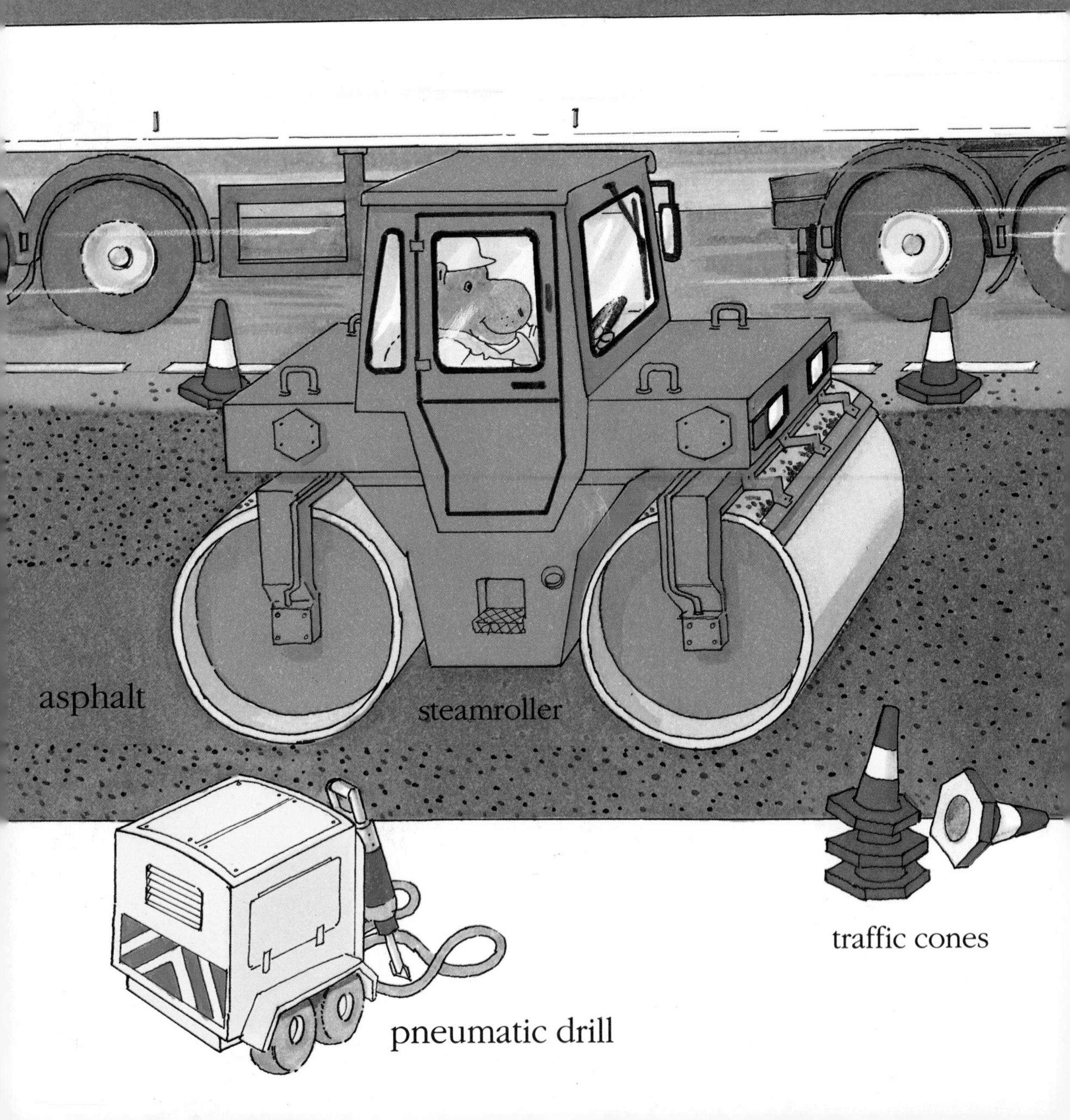
asphalt
steamroller
traffic cones
pneumatic drill

Heavy traffic on main roads and highways can wear away the road's surface. Frost and snow sometimes cause cracking.

Bernie is tired and hungry. He's driven most of the journey, so there's time to stop for a meal with his truck-driver friends.

Arnie's
CAFE

Back on the road, the steering doesn't feel quite right, so Bernie pulls over by the side of the road.

It's a flat tire. He calls a repair truck on the CB.

The repair truck comes quickly. The mechanic removes the flat tire.

Then he puts on a new tire. Bernie will make his delivery in time after all.

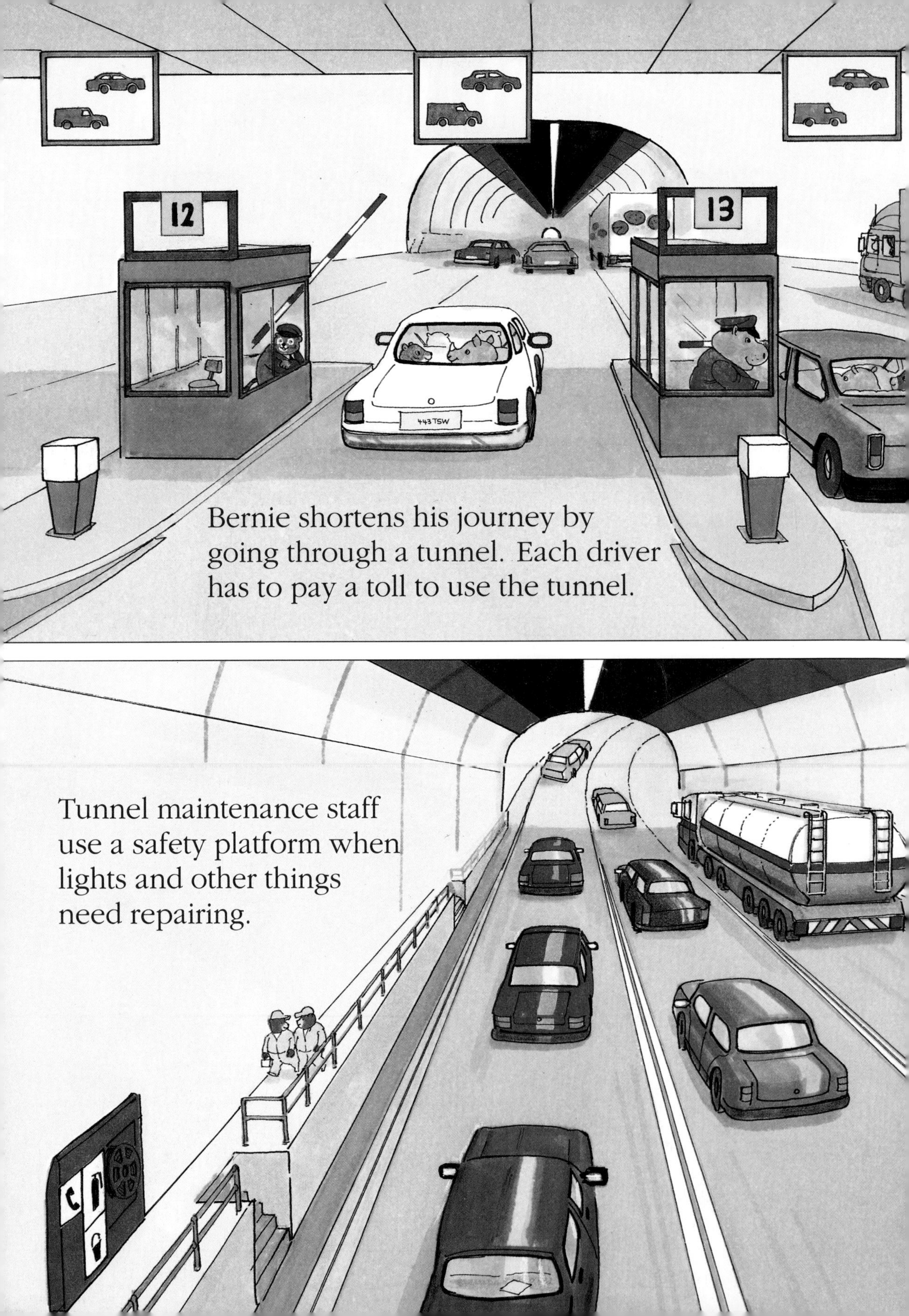

Bernie shortens his journey by going through a tunnel. Each driver has to pay a toll to use the tunnel.

Tunnel maintenance staff use a safety platform when lights and other things need repairing.

Toll tunnels and toll bridges can often save drivers extra miles of driving.

This tunnel goes under a wide river. Each vehicle must stay in its own lane and obey the speed limit.

Back at the trucking office they get a phone call: "Can someone pick up a load from the docks?" The boss radios Bernie. "Sure," says Bernie, and he's really glad. No truck driver likes to drive back without another load.

At the docks, Bernie's truck is unloaded. The soft drink cases are checked to make sure that nothing is missing.

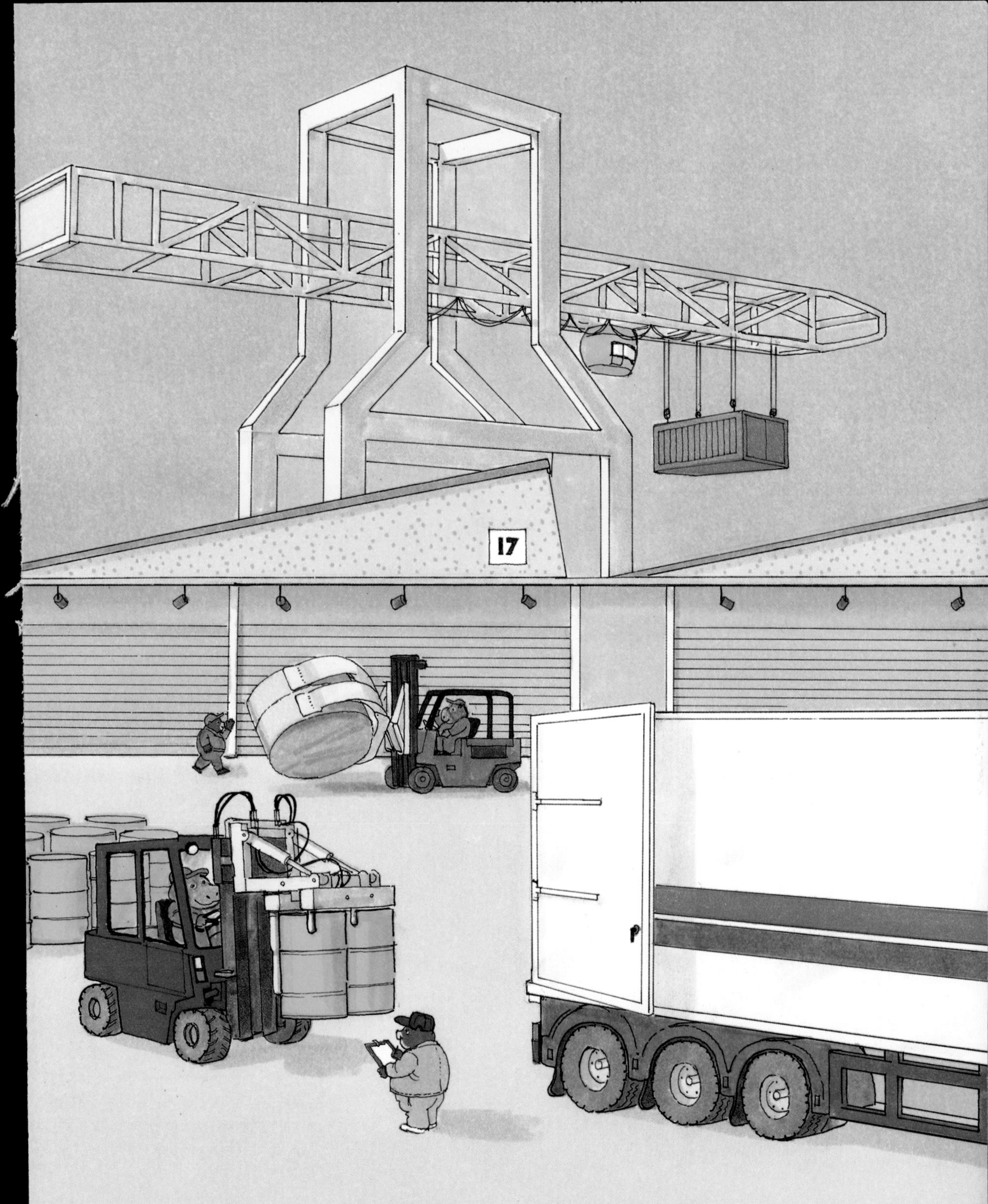

Then Bernie checks his return load: molasses in large metal drums. It takes a while to load the trailer, so he calls home to say he'll be a little late.

But he still gets home in time to say good night.